His Miracle

by
Euryia Larsen

Description

Sienna Jensen

Bah Humbug! That is what I think of Christmas this year. Having recently broken up with my fiance and lost my job all in the same week would put anyone in a sour mood. Realizing you're spending Christmas utterly alone turns you into the Grinch. So I'll eat my Chinese Food and watch blow 'em up movies and it'll all be good, maybe.

Alec "Nomad" Hunter

My club President sent me out to meet with the Christmas Falls President to work out an alliance. That leaves me in this small town where they know how to do Christmas. I'm checking out the town square when the cutest Grinch I've ever met crashes into me, literally. I know instantly that she's my Christmas miracle, but can I be hers? Can I convince her to pack up her life and trust in me to be all she needs and wants?

Chapter 1

Sienna

Bah Humbug! That's what I thought of Christmas this year. I pulled my coat tighter around my body as a sharp wind cut through me. No matter how much I wanted to forget this past week it seemed determined to sit front and center in my thoughts.

Monday started as a typical Monday, nothing great and nothing terrible. When I finally arrived home to the apartment I shared with my fiancé, Daniel, I knew something was off before I even opened the front door. I was surprised to see Daniel home before me, only he wasn't alone. Sitting on his lap was his "assistant", Cindy.

We were getting married in less than a month, and our apartment was wedding central with boxes and stuff everywhere. My eyes blinked as I watched as Cindy quickly stood and fixed her bra. I was so excited to marry this man that my brain struggled to comprehend what I was seeing.

Daniel and I had been together for nearly two years. While things weren't perfect, we loved each other through thick and thin. He'd help me in the areas I was lacking to become a better version of myself. I'd lost weight, started wearing the clothes he wanted me to, and moved up the social ladder. While I didn't have time to do the things I loved, like painting, Daniel was happy which made me happy. But if he was happy, why was Cindy on his lap?

"Daniel…" I whispered in desperation. The horror and shock before me left me in a dazed state of mind. Everything felt frozen.

"Shit! Sienna, baby. It's not what it looks like," Daniel tried to explain.

"How long?" My voice was hoarse. My mind was stuck on trying to understand.

"Cindy was just helping…"

"HOW. LONG. DANIEL."

"Six months."

"Why on God's green earth did you propose to me while having an affair with her?" My voice took on an exasperated tone. "If you were that miserable with me why didn't you just break it off?"

"You are the perfect wife in the eyes of the partners. Cindy is my assistant."

"Well, I guess you're just shit out of luck then." I walked into my bedroom and quickly pulled out a travel bag and filled it with enough to get me by.

"Sienna, wait. Let's talk about this."

"Fuck you!" All I could think of was getting out of there. I grabbed my purse and shoving Daniel out of the way, ran out to my car. I didn't know where I was going or what I was going to do. I just drove.

Finally, I found a decent hotel and got a room. Sitting on the classically hard bed, I just sat there and tried to figure out what I did wrong. I must have fallen asleep at some point. I woke up to the alarm on my phone going off. I needed to get ready for work.

My brain was in the aftermath of a bomb going off. There was a continual ringing, nothing made sense, and my emotions seemed frozen. I couldn't think straight.

Somehow I managed to look semi-decent and made my way to my car. The drive to work was short for which I was eternally thankful. When I walked in everyone went quiet. It felt off but then everything felt off, truth be told.

Just as I settled in at my cubicle I heard, "Ms. Jensen, a word."

With a deep sigh, I hung my head. The spirit of Christmas was determined to hand me a big ole 'Fuck you'. I wouldn't even be surprised if coal showed up at this point.

I walked into Mr. Williams' office with a smile that I didn't feel plastered to my face. "What can I do for you?"

"Close the door and sit down," my boss ordered without even looking at me. The twists in my stomach knew this wasn't going to be a good meeting. After closing his office door, I sat down in one of the chairs in front of his desk.

"Ms. Jensen, today will be your last day. We've been asked to trim the budget and since you were the last to be hired, unfortunately, you're the first to be let go. Knowing this season it's hard to find employment, you will receive two months' pay as severance. Please gather your things."

I sat blinking at him. I'd just been fired days before Christmas. What the fucking level of hell was I in?

Before I even realized it, a box of my stuff sat in my passenger seat, and I was driving. I stopped driving when I saw that I was in the center of town surrounded by everything beautiful about Christmas in Christmas Falls.

I just sat there and all the emotions hit at once. After a bit, I silently took stock of my life. My car was my own. My bank account was still my own. I didn't have a place to live or a job, but the money I did have was still my own.

Wiping my face, I took a deep calming breath and decided to take a walk through all the decorations. Maybe it could lighten my heart and give me some joy. I swung open my car door before I realized anyone was walking by.

In slow motion, I watched as it slammed into the back of a man nearly knocking him off his feet. When he righted himself and turned to look at me with a disgruntled look I swallowed nervously. Standing there was the largest, most gorgeous man I'd ever seen.

Chapter 2

Nomad

Christmas Falls. The name of the town said it all. This was Christmas done right, definitely bordering on Christmas overload. I drove past the town to the Christmas Falls MC clubhouse. My club, the Dragon Skulls MC, we're expanding some of our operations. Saint, my President, had worked out a great alliance deal with Red, the President of Christmas Falls MC.

Normally Saint would have come himself or had Red travel to us. But this time of year there was too much going on and Saint's Ole Lady needed him there. As the club's Nomad, it was my job to do what needed to be done away from home.

I was considering settling down though. The idea of settling down alone didn't sit well. I was tired of being alone and only sleeping with nameless one-nighters.

With a shake of my head, I parked my bike and walked up to the clubhouse door. It sounded like a party was happening. I sighed as I hoped we could get our meeting over and done with. I wanted a comfortable bed, a hot shower and maybe watch a little Diehard on the television.

"Nomad! Welcome!" A large man with a red beard wore a broad smile as he approached. It was obvious why this man went by Red.

I shook his hand as I approached him. "Red! Great town you have here. It definitely gets into the holiday spirit."

Red's laugh was as loud as you would expect from a man his size. "A town named Christmas Falls not having holiday spirit is like chocolate chip cookies without the chocolate chips... horrifying!"

I couldn't help but laugh at this man. What made me laugh even harder was the thought of Saint doing business with him. When it came to business, Saint was intense. Growing up without basics like food and clothing ingrained in him how important it was to take making money seriously. His role as MC President was never taken lightly and as a result, the club's loyalty was never questioned.

Red led me inside to his office and as we sat down he said, "Knowing Saint as I do, he won't be able to relax and enjoy the holidays until all business is handled."

"That is correct. Here are the contracts, signed by Saint. Read over them, nothing has been changed but don't just take my word for it. Once signed I'll deliver a copy back to Saint and then it's all settled."

I sat back as Red read over every page before signing it. Once the last pages were signed he handed both copies to me to verify everything was in order. With a broad smile, I affixed each contract with the official Dragon Skulls seal and handed one copy back to Red. "It was a pleasure doing business with you."

"You're welcome to stay and have a few drinks with us," Red offered.

"I'm going to call Saint and get everything in order before grabbing some dinner and getting some sleep. Drove a lot of miles today."

"I hear ya. My back can't handle the long rides like I used to. Getting old fucking sucks."

"That it does, that it does."

I hung out for a few more minutes with ole Red before I headed out to my bike. Clicking the button for Saint's number I didn't have to wait for him to pick up. "Nomad, what's the word?"

"All signed and stamped. I'm gonna pick up some chow and settle in for the night. These long rides get harder and harder."

"Thank you for handling this business. Whenever you're ready to settle in, you have a home waiting for you."

"I appreciate that, boss. I'll see you in a couple of days. Merry Christmas."

"Be safe, Nomad."

I turned on my bike and decided to head back into town to find some food and a room to crash in. Parking my bike, I looked around town with a smile. The decorations were classy and beautiful. It brought to mind memories of Christmases past before life went to shit.

Climbing off my bike I decided to take a walk to find some food. I was so distracted by the decorations and lights I didn't notice the lady sitting in the car as I walked by. Suddenly, what felt like a car door slammed into me from behind. As soon as I righted myself I turned around to see who attacked me. On the other side of the offending door was the most beautiful lady I'd ever seen.

Chapter 3

Sienna

I climbed out of my car and immediately asked, "Are you okay? I'm so sorry. I should have looked before wildly opening my door like that."

"I'm fine. Are you alright? It looks like some asshole has upset you. A woman as beautiful as you should never be treated badly."

I blinked at his charming words. I expected him to be mad, not charming. Certainly not concerned about me looking upset. "You look busy and my depressing state of affairs would only ruin your evening and waste too much of your time."

"My plans only consisted of going for a walk to find food and going to my hotel room to watch a good Christmas movie classic like Die Hard."

I started to laugh before tears started falling and a sob escaped. "T-that was my plan until my life went straight down the toilet."

Before I realized it, he was guiding me over to a bench and sitting down next to me. "The name is Alec but everyone calls me Nomad. I'm just here for the night but I'm already considering lengthening my stay if it means getting to know you."

I could feel my cheeks turning pink at his sweet words. "It's nice to meet you Alec aka Nomad. I'm Sienna and I don't know what I'm doing."

"I have all the time in the world and a spare shoulder with your name on it. Heck, you never know, you might feel better just telling someone."

I nodded before I took a deep breath to calm my emotions. "I worked a boring office job but it paid well. After work yesterday I came home to find my fiancé of six months home early and not alone. His assistant was with him. He admitted the only reason he was with me was that I looked good to the partners and he wanted to get a coveted promotion."

"So he was cheating on you with his secretary? What a cliche douchbag. How long was he cheating for?"

I sighed as I wiped away a tear that had escaped. "Longer than we'd been engaged. I was hurt but what's even sadder is that I also feel relieved. I've known something was off for a while. I just didn't want to think about it."

"Then I'm happy for you, but the look on your face doesn't say relief."

"Today I got laid off from work. So now I'm homeless because I was sharing an apartment with Daniel, jobless, and completely alone for Christmas. I'll be eating Chinese food and watching Christmas movies in a hotel room. I have no clue what I'm going to do next and I feel beat up and depressed all rolled together."

"Well, now you're not alone. You'll be spending Christmas with me as my very own Christmas miracle. As for what's next, that's easy, you're coming with me to get Chinese food and then we'll go back to either your room or mine and watch some Die Hard. Nothing like a good Bruce Willis Christmas movie to cheer us up."

"Oh no! I couldn't do that. Being with me will just ruin your evening and holiday."

"Sienna, have you ever heard of love at first sight?"

"That's the stuff of romance novels and movie fantasies." I looked at him like he was crazy. What did silly romance notions have to do with me?

He took my hand and gave me a smile that practically turned me into a puddle of goo. "I used to think so, too. Then I saw it happen to my club President and several other powerful men that I know and respect. We've known each other for what, five minutes?"

I nodded, finding myself wanting to hear what he said next. "Not long."

"Not long at all, and yet the moment my eyes met yours a voice in my head said, 'Mine.' I'm sure that's all caveman sounding but the more we talk the more I feel the truth in that voice. We're both alone, both at a time of potential change in our lives. Spend the evening with me. Get to know who I am and maybe we won't have to be alone anymore."

I looked at him and thought about what he said. As crazy as it sounded, it felt like there was truth there as well. Daniel almost felt like an inconsequential blip in my life that was leading me to this man. "I think I'd like that."

Nomad and I walked around town viewing the decorations as we learned about each other. I learned about the motorcycle club he was a part of and he learned about me. He learned how I used to love Christmas, how I loved to read and loved to create art. I learned how he lost his family before finding a new one.

The more I learned about him the more I liked. Eventually, we decided on Chinese takeout and went back to my hotel suite to eat and watch movies. It was late at night before we fell asleep watching the final Die Hard movie. I fell asleep with a smile on my face, knowing that I'd had the best time with Nomad and didn't want it to end. I could only hope he'd be there when I woke up.

Nomad

I woke up holding the most beautiful creature in my arms. She looked so peaceful as she slept. A small smile graced her pink lips. She was it for me. I knew it the moment my eyes met hers. It was as if our souls joined together after a long separation.

It was Christmas Eve and I planned to spend the whole day with my beautiful Sienna. I was hoping that I could convince them to travel back to Texas with me. At some point last evening, I just knew without a shadow of a doubt that I wanted to settle down and leave the nomadic life with her. With my Christmas miracle. Now I just needed to convince her.

I tenderly brushed her hair away from her face and smiled. In my heart, I was already in love with this angel. It sounded crazy but it was no less true. This woman was mine. She was my soul mate, my love, my everything.

I watched as she stretched her body out along mine and blinked her eyes open with a smile. "Hi," she whispered.

"Hi, baby. Sleep well?"

"Wonderfully. They were filled with dreams of a hot biker." Her smile turned mischievous as she added, "I hope that doesn't make you too jealous."

I smirked at the fun twinkle in her eye. "Well, I'll have to take him out as an obvious threat. There is only one hot biker that should ever be in your dreams, beautiful."

"Oh?"

"What was this biker like?"

"Well, he was gorgeous and big. He made me laugh and feel beautiful. He was the man I've been waiting for. You know, he looked a lot like you. Crazy."

"Crazy indeed." I immediately pinned Sienna to me and started to tickle her as she squealed and giggled as she tried to escape the torture of my fingers. I finally held her tightly to me on my lap as we stared at each other and caught our breath. I wanted to kiss this girl. I wanted to make her mine.

Chapter 4

Sienna

A loud growl emitted from my stomach as we stared at each other. I was hoping he'd kiss me. I so desperately wanted him to kiss me.

"You must be starving."

I'd completely forgotten about my stomach and food, but he was right. I was starving, and just not for food. Sitting up, I ran my fingers over his stubbled cheek. "Nomad," I whispered, leaning in closer. "Kiss me."

With a groan he pulled me closer, kissing me with a hunger that matched my own. I ran my fingers through his silky hair and moaned when his tongue caressed mine. His cock pressed against my ass, but instead of fear and nervousness, all I felt was anticipation and a deep need. "Please," I begged.

He smiled against my lips as he lifted me and positioned me so I was straddling him. When he lowered me down so his hard length was pressing right against my aching pussy, I moaned and started to grind against him.

"Relax, baby. I've got you. I'll always keep you safe."

I gave a quick nod, trusting him at his word, and rocked my hips harder against him. "But I want you to take me to bed." I ran my tongue over his bottom lip before I gave it a soft bite. "I want you inside me."

He groaned and cupped my ass, giving it a hard squeeze. "God, I love hearing you say that, and I'll gladly give you my cock, baby, but first I want you to come on my lap. Grind against me, beautiful. Take your pleasure."

Bracing my hands against his broad shoulders, I moved my body, grateful I decided on yoga pants today under my skirt. The thin fabric was letting me feel everything, and the friction was so fucking delicious. I threw my head back and gasped, working my hips harder, shamelessly using him for my own pleasure.

He let out a deep groan, bringing one hand up to lift my shirt and roughly push my bra aside. As soon as my breast was exposed, he tongued my nipple and filled his mouth. "You're so fucking sexy, baby," he murmured against my skin, teasing me with his mouth until I felt my orgasm quickly approaching.

Nomad felt me tense, and when I moaned his name, he grabbed my ass, digging his fingers in and moving me even harder against him as I exploded from the inside out. My body shattered as I whimpered while the thick, hard cock beneath me was so close but not nearly close enough.

Desperately needing to taste him, I pulled his head back, my mouth claiming his in a greedy, desperate kiss. "Nomad," I begged against his lips. "Please."

With a groan, he wrapped his arms tightly around me and stood up, carrying me like I weighed nothing. I kissed his neck, nipping at his skin and running my tongue over his neck. By the time he reached the bed, I was so drunk on lust I could barely think.

He gently lowered me to the bed and stilled my hands which were practically ripping the buttons off his jeans. "Look at me, baby," he murmured, cupping my face and meeting my eyes. "Are you sure? I don't want to push you into doing something you aren't ready for."

"Yes, I'm sure, handsome. I want this. I want you, all of you."

His eyes darkened at my words, and I knew he was forcing himself to hold back, not wanting to scare me. "Promise me you'll stop me if you feel uncomfortable. No matter what, baby."

"I will. I promise," I said in a breathy rush, confident that I wouldn't need to.

Satisfied that I wanted this, he let go of my hands so I could get back to undressing him. Smiling at my impatience when I let out a frustrated groan, he pulled back, taking over with his steady hands, and made quick work of taking off his clothes. Soon he was naked and looking down at me like a starving man. He was fully erect, his cock covered in a bead of precum.

Running his hands up my legs, he hooked his fingers under the waist of my skirt and leggings, and slowly slid them off, taking my panties with them. When I was naked from the waist down, he grabbed my thighs and parted them, letting out a string of curses as I laid open before him.

Nomad let go of my thighs just long enough to pull my shirt off and unclasp my bra before he grabbed them again. Parting my legs in a way that completely exposed me to his hungry gaze, he said, "You're the most beautiful woman I've ever seen, baby." His Texas accent was thicker than usual, and the sound of it had me rocking my hips up in invitation. He smiled and slid one hand up my thigh before slowly dragging his finger along my slit. "You're so wet for me, baby."

"Nomad," I moaned. My heart raced even faster when he very slowly started to slide one finger into me.

"I need to get you ready for me. I'm going to work your pussy and make you come baby, so you're nice and open for me."

I gripped the bedding and let out a whimper of pure pleasure when he lowered his head and ran his tongue over my swollen clit as he gently slid another finger in. Letting go of the blanket, I grabbed his head instead, biting my lip as he sucked on my clit and stretched me with his fingers. The mix of sensations had me squirming beneath him and breathing heavily, feeling the orgasm that was just out of reach.

One more firm lick of his tongue sent me over the edge, and when I moaned his name, he slid a third finger into me, spreading me wider and finger-fucking me through my release. My whole body shook beneath him and went slack as I tried to catch my breath, slowly coming back to reality. He kept his fingers inside me while he rimmed my clit, sending aftershocks through every part of my body.

"Alec," I moaned, grabbing onto his shoulders and trying to pull him up to me so I could kiss him and feel his skin against mine.

He hovered his lips above my skin, licking and nipping his way up my stomach and chest, stopping to give each nipple a soft bite before finally bringing his lips to mine. His fingers were still buried inside me, working me gently as he parted my lips with his tongue and delved inside, claiming every inch of my mouth as his.

I dug my heels into the mattress and rocked up to him, kissing him hard and wrapping my arms around him.

Pulling his fingers out, he pressed the head of his cock against my slit. "Are you sure?" he asked one last time, and I loved him so much at that moment. He was desperate to be inside me. I saw the raw need in his eyes and the tense way he was holding his body. His swollen dick was dripping pre-cum onto me, and still, he waited for me to tell him I'm okay.

"I love you," I whispered, running my tongue over his lips. "I need you inside me, Alec."

"I love you, too, baby, so fucking much." He kissed me gently and cupped the back of my head, bringing his other hand down to grasp my hip as he slowly slid into me. His thick head spread me wide. Even with the prep work, his size was still a shock.

I clenched around him, making it impossible for him to go in any further without having to slam into me. "Just relax, baby."

I nodded and clung to him even harder. He placed his thumb on my clit, slowly working me while he kissed me harder, making me forget about everything except how good he was making me feel. He flooded my body with so much pleasure and love, not leaving room for anything else, including doubt.

Feeling my body start to tense, he smiled against my lips. "That's right, baby. Come around my cock." His words were enough to have me bucking up against him as the orgasm slammed into me. My pussy clenched around his head, but as soon as I started to relax, he slid completely into me, flooding my body with the perfect mix of pleasure and pain.

His deep groan vibrated against my chest as his kiss turned harder and hungrier, and I felt my lust start to take over. I urged him with my body for more, digging my nails into his back and my heels into his ass, but he resisted, keeping himself still inside me. "Nomad," I growled. "Please!"

He let out a soft laugh and looked down at me. His eyes were a mix of love, lust, and worry. I cupped his face, smoothing his worried brow. "I'm perfect."

He smiled and kissed me softly. "God, your pussy feels amazing. You are amazing."

Having him inside me was better than I ever thought possible. With Alec's powerful body on top of mine and his cock stretching me right to the cusp of being too much, all I felt was an all-consuming love and ecstasy. I lost myself to him completely. Dragging my nails down his back, I rocked my hips up to meet his thrusts and deepened the kiss, sucking his tongue into my mouth and pulling a deep groan from him.

His hand slid under my ass, cupping one of my cheeks and tilting me up so he could go even deeper. The sensation had me moaning into his mouth and digging my nails into his back, urging him for more. He slammed into me even harder, making my eyes roll back in my head as he showed me exactly what he was capable of.

I gave myself over to him, letting him fuck me as hard and fast as he wanted, because every single thing he wanted to do to me, I wanted it too. Each hard thrust made my nipples scrape along his sweaty chest, sending little sparks of pleasure all through me. I tightened my legs around him, knowing I was close, giving his bottom lip a suck as the ecstasy built.

One more hard thrust had me screaming his name and clenching so tightly around him that he had no choice but to join me. He moaned my name as his cock pulsed and he lost himself in his release. His thumb stroked my cheek while he kissed me gently, slowing everything down until we were both completely spent.

I felt him smile against my lips before he pulled back enough to rest his forehead against mine. "I love you, Sienna."

"I love you, Alec." I gave a big sigh and raised my arms in a stretch. "Wow."

He laughed and gave my ass one last squeeze before raising onto his forearms so he could see me better. "Are you okay? Any regrets?"

"I'm better than okay, and definitely no regrets." When he started to pull out, I tightened my legs, trying to hold him in place. "Wait, not yet."

He gave me a sweet smile and in one quick motion flipped us so that I was on top. I rested my head on his chest, listening to the steady beat of his heart as he grew soft inside me. "I don't ever want this to end," I admitted in a whisper. "I wish we could stay like this forever."

His fingers danced along my spine, and I could hear the amusement in his voice when he said, "I'm more than happy to do this again anytime you want. Wake me up if you need to. I'll happily lose sleep if it means I get to be inside you again."

I smiled at the idea of waking him up by straddling him and sliding down his length until he was fully seated inside me. My fingers lightly danced along his chest.

"Come on, baby. You need to eat something."

Knowing he was right, I only protested a little bit when he slid me off him. He gave me a sweet, lingering kiss before getting up and coming back with a warm cloth. I'm surprised when he gently parts my legs and pressed the cloth against my sore pussy, soothing and cleaning me. I couldn't help the small wince when I moved slightly and felt the sting of what just happened.

"Fuck, baby, I'm sorry." I grabbed onto his wrist, hating the worry I heard in his voice.

"I'm just a little sore, Nomad, but I'm guessing that's to be expected. You're huge. I knew it was going to hurt a little, but I wanted this to happen, and it's a good pain, not a bad one."

He still looked worried, but he gave me a nod and slowly moved the cloth away. Bending lower, he brought his mouth to my swollen pussy, slowly kissing every inch of me until the discomfort is a distant memory.

"You sure do know how to treat a girl," I said while a lazy grin spread across my face.

I feel the heat of his breath on my skin when he says, "I know how to treat you, baby."

Reaching down, I cupped his gorgeous face and pulled him up to me. Being around Alec was so easy. His good looks were still a bit intimidating to me, but he was so down to earth that I couldn't help relaxing around him and just having a good time.

His face turned serious as he looked towards the television. "I don't know how you feel about kids. I don't know if you want them or not, but if we do have them, I only want them with you. I want everything with you."

I smiled and looked at my very own Christmas miracle. He looked nervous, as if what he said was too much too fast and it was the cutest thing I'd ever seen. "Do you know how cute you are right now? You seem so nervous."

"I'm not nervous," he insisted. "I just really hope you want kids because after what I just filled you with, chances are high that we're going to have one."

"I didn't even think about you wearing a condom. To be honest I didn't want anything between us. I would've stopped you if I'd been worried about it. I just, I don't know, I liked the idea of you coming inside me."

He let out a soft groan and held me tighter against his side. "You're the only woman I've ever come inside," he admitted. "I couldn't stand the thought of something between us either. But if you'd rather not take the risk, I understand, baby."

25

I leaned closer and gave his bottom lip a soft nip. "I like you coming inside me." He groaned and pulled me into his lap so I could feel how hard I was making him.

"The only thing that's stopping me from burying myself inside you again is knowing you need to eat. It is tempting, though."

I smiled and laughed when he wrapped his arms around me and captured my lips in a passionate kiss. I lose myself in my biker, making him laugh when I slid my hand down his joggers so I could grab onto the sculpted ass.

Epilogue

Nomad

We spent the day in bed, making plans for the future in between exploring each other's bodies. It was the best Christmas Eve I could ever remember. One that I would never have dreamed of happening.

Christmas Day entailed waiting for Daniel to leave the apartment before going to get everything Sienna wanted and needed. It didn't take very long to fill her car with several suitcases and bins along with the few pieces of furniture that were important to her. The rest we would get new for our house together.

We drove back to Texas where I was excited to introduce Sienna to my family. She was immediately welcomed and was even accepted by Saint after they spent some time talking. It didn't take long before I started to plan. I had two important questions I wanted to ask her.

Several days later we were having breakfast at the local diner. The whole club was there for what I hoped was a special event. A special strawberry cake with chocolate-covered strawberries decorating it appeared on our table much to Sienna's surprise. I took that moment of distraction and bent down on one knee in front of my girl.

"Sienna, my Christmas miracle, my heart is yours completely. You're my soulmate and my partner. You're the greatest Christmas gift I've ever been blessed with. Make this ole biker happy and say you'll become my ole lady."

Sienna's squeal of surprise and joy as she yelled, "Yes! Yes! Yes!" made me smile so big I was sure my face was going to break.

After placing her property cut on her I continued to my second question, "Now that you're my ole lady, make it official and say you'll be my wife as well?"

As I showed her the beautiful pink diamond heart that matched her perfectly, Sienna threw herself at me, landing kisses all over my face as she said, "Yes!" Over and over again.

Our life would continue to get better and better each year we were together.

THE END

About the Author

Euryia Larsen grew up thinking that what she was being told about the world was only part of the story. She loves myths both historical and modern and often sees the possibility in 'what if'. A good romance with strong 'alpha' heroes and even stronger heroines that can be partners for them are her favorite kinds of books. If the heroines are just a tad crazy, even better.

Euryia is a stay-at-home mom of two beautiful daughters, three crazy cats, three crazier dogs, and a husband to round out the bunch. She deals with her fair share of issues while dealing with Fibromyalgia and other complications and as a result, she finds an escape in books where there is always a happily ever after. She's always been creative and has written for herself as an audience for longer than she can remember.

I'd love to hear your thoughts on this or myths or books in general or even just a hello.

Check me out at
http://www.EuryiaLarsen.com
or feel free to email me at
EuryiaLarsenAuthor@gmail.com

Other Books by Euryia Larsen

Broken Butterfly Dreams

Standalone Novellas:

The Mobster's Violet

Clover's Luck

Touch of Gluttony

Halloween Darkness

Another Notch On Her Toolbelt

Sealed With A Kiss

Fate's Surprise

Midnight Rose

His Curvy Housemaid

Hello, Goodbye

The Dark Side (Dragon Skulls MC):

Saint

Beautiful Smile

Twisted Savior

Belladonna Club:

To Trap A Kiss

His Peridot

Zima Family:

Devil's Desire

Cursed Angel

Baranov Bratva:

Sinful Duty

Sweet Child of Mine

Menage Series:

Masked Surprise

Sweet Cherry Pie

Home on the Ranch

Perfect Storm

Curveball

Lonesome Shadows

Cursed Guardians

Love is Love Boxsets:

Menage A Trois

Affaire de Coeur

Not the Good Guy (Kazon Brothers)

with Kyra Nyx:

Kazon Brothers Box Set

The Dark

The Beast

The Villain

Saga of The Realms:

Power of Love – Prequel Novella (Paperback)

Power of Love – Prequel Novella (Free Ebook)

Bonded By Destiny

War of Giants

Printed in Great Britain
by Amazon

61522391R00020